Metalmiss

'Come on, Dad,' urged the twins, 'Tell us.'

'That's enough, Ted,' said Mrs Potter. 'Stop teasing. Put them out of their misery.'

'All right,' laughed Mr Potter. 'The answer is . . . *yes*. You *are* going to have your robot teacher.'

'Fantastic!' yelled Holly. She jumped off her chair and danced around the room, chanting. 'A robot for 3R. A robot for 3R.'

Mrs Potter was looking at Harry, who had said nothing but had turned a little pale.

'You'll like it, Harry,' she said reassuringly. 'I'm sure you will.'

'Wish I was so sure,' said Harry glumly, as he went off to pack his schoolbag.

Linda Pitt

METALMISS

Illustrated by Paul Dowling

RED FOX

A Red Fox Book

Published by Random House Children's Books
20 Vauxhall Bridge Road, London SW1V 2SA

A division of Random House UK Ltd
London Melbourne Sydney Auckland
Johannesburg and agencies throughout the world

First published in 1991 by Andersen Press Ltd

Red Fox edition 1994

3 5 7 9 10 8 6 4 2

Printed and bound in Great Britain by
Cox & Wyman Ltd, Reading, Berkshire

RANDOM HOUSE UK Limited Reg. No. 954009

ISBN 0 09 997290 5

Chapter 1

'Never heard such a racket!' complained Mrs Green, the cleaning lady at Pinkerton Primary School. 'Call themselves teachers! Worse than the children, they are.'

'You're right there,' agreed Mr Clarke, the caretaker. 'Ought to be ashamed of themselves, shouting like that. Just as well the kids have all gone home!'

They were standing in classroom 4, just above the staffroom. Below them, a staff meeting was taking place. It was a very noisy meeting – very noisy indeed.

'Mind you, they've never been as bad as that

before,' Mr Clarke admitted, shaking his head. 'Wonder what's going on!'

Had he and Mrs Green known what was going on, they would have been *very* surprised.

Mr Clegg, the headmaster, had a louder voice than any of the other teachers. At last he managed to make himself heard.

'Quiet!' he yelled, in a voice usually reserved for an assembly hall full of noisy children. He was red faced and angry.

The teachers were startled into silence. He had never shouted at *them* like that before.

'Now!' barked Mr Clegg, his face practically purple. 'Hands up! One at a time!'

Meekly, the teachers obeyed.

'Mr Jones, could we hear from you first, please?'

Mr Jones, the deputy head, stood up. He was a tall, grey-haired man who had taught at the school for many years. 'I'm sure that I speak for all of us,' he said firmly, 'when I say that we will *never* accept a robot teacher at Pinkerton School.'

As he sat down there was loud applause and cries of 'Hear! Hear!'

'Very well,' said Mr Clegg grimly. 'That seems to be that. Is there anyone in the room who does *not* agree with Mr Jones?'

There was silence.

'In that case,' said Mr Clegg, writing busily on a notepad, 'I will convey your views to the…'

'Mr Clegg, could I just…?' The voice tailed off as the headmaster looked up irritably.

'Yes, Miss Bird, what is it?'

At the back of the room, little Miss Bird stood up. Everyone stared.

She cleared her throat nervously. 'I would just like to say…to say that I do not altogether agree with Mr Jones.'

There were gasps of amazement. Miss Bird was new to the school. So far, she had never been known to disagree with anyone.

'It seems to me,' continued Miss Bird in a stronger voice, 'that since Mrs Riley is leaving and a teacher cannot be found to take her class next term, we should at least *try* this robot. I think it could be quite exciting – for the children – *and* for us.'

With that, Miss Bird sat down. No one spoke.

Mr Clegg looked around the room. For the first time that afternoon he was actually smiling.

'As you all know,' he said, 'I am inclined to agree with Miss Bird. I think we should try it out. After all, what have we got to lose?'

'Only our jobs,' muttered young Mr Roberts. 'Might turn out to be better than any of us.'

'Don't be silly!' snapped Mr Clegg. 'This is a machine – not a person.'

'Only joking,' said Mr Roberts hastily. 'In fact, I rather like the idea of a robot for 3R.'

'So do I,' said Mrs Riley, 3R's teacher. 'It *is* only for one term – and I suppose you could get rid of it straight away if it turned out to be a disaster. Couldn't you, Mr Clegg?'

'Of course,' agreed Mr Clegg.

The discussion continued, some for, some against, until Mr Jones stood up again. He was looking very serious.

'Mr Clegg, did you say that Holly and Harry Potter's grandfather invented these robots?'

'Yes. Professor Potter works at the university. So far his machines have only been used in factories and offices. But when he heard that the twins would be without a teacher next term, he offered to design a robot to fill the gap.'

'Are the Potter twins those two red-headed children?' asked Miss Bird.

'Yes,' said Mrs Riley. 'Bright red hair and bright blue eyes. You can't miss them.'

'Would the matter be discussed with the parents of the other children in 3R?' asked Mr Jones.

'Certainly,' said Mr Clegg. 'There would be a meeting for all the parents – a meeting with Professor Potter and Mr Robertson from the Education Office.'

'In that case,' said Mr Jones, 'I would like to say that I have changed my mind. *If* the parents agree and *if* it is only for one term, I am prepared to accept this robot.'

And so, after some more discussion, it was decided. Next term, if the parents agreed, 3R would have its robot teacher.

Chapter 2

'Gran,' said Harry Potter anxiously, as he and his grandmother settled down on the sofa to watch TV, 'Grandpa's robot wouldn't be a scary one, would it?'

He spoke softly because his twin sister, Holly, was in the kitchen making tea. He did not want her to hear.

Granny understood. 'No dear,' she said, quietly but firmly. 'If your grandpa designs a robot it won't be a scary one. You don't need to worry.'

'Who's worried?' demanded Holly, staggering in from the kitchen with a heavy tray. She always liked to make the tea when Granny came to babysit. 'He's not still fussing about the robot, is he?'

'I'm not fussing,' Harry protested. 'I just want to know what it's going to be like, that's all.'

'And very sensible too,' Granny said soothingly. She took the tray from Holly and placed it carefully on a low table. 'After all, you'd want to know what *any* new teacher was going to be like.'

'I bet we won't get it anyway,' said Holly. 'Norma Nicolson's mum will never want a robot teaching her precious Norma.'

'We'll have to wait and see,' said Granny. 'Your grandpa's explaining all about it at tonight's meeting. Then it's up to the parents to decide.'

'Bet the meeting will go on and on,' said Harry. 'Don't suppose *we'll* know until the morning.'

The meeting did go on and on. Harry tried hard to stay awake but the twins were both fast asleep when their parents and grandfather returned.

Next morning Harry was so sleepy that it was breakfast time before he remembered. He hardly dared to ask.

'What...what did they decide about the robot, Dad?'

'The robot!' exclaimed Holly. 'Do you know, I'd forgotten all about it. Are we going to get it, Dad?'

'I thought you'd never ask,' grinned Mr Potter. 'But since you're not in any *real* hurry to know, I'll just make another pot of tea before I tell you about it.'

He winked at Mrs Potter as he went into the kitchen.

'Mum,' urged Holly, '*you* tell us. Go on, Mum – *please*.'

'No,' Mrs Potter shook her head, 'you'll have to wait until your father has made the tea.'

Slowly Mr Potter came in and sat down. Slowly he poured out the tea.

'Come on, Dad,' urged the twins, 'tell us.'

'That's enough, Ted,' said Mrs Potter. 'Stop teasing. Put them out of their misery.'

'All right,' laughed Mr Potter. 'The answer is...*yes*. You *are* going to have your robot teacher.'

'Fantastic!' yelled Holly. She jumped off her chair and danced around the room, chanting, 'A robot for 3R. A robot for 3R.'

Mrs Potter was looking at Harry, who had said nothing but had turned a little pale.

'You'll like it, Harry,' she said reassuringly. 'I'm sure you will.'

'Wish I was so sure,' said Harry glumly, as he went off to pack his schoolbag.

At school there was great excitement, especially in Room 6 – 3R's classroom.

'Well,' said Mrs Riley, 'it looks as if you've all heard about your new teacher.'

'Yes, Mrs Riley,' they chorused.

'And are you all happy about it?'

Each child had something to say.

'My dad thinks it's fantastic.'

'My mum doesn't. She thinks it's really scary.'

'I think it's really scary as well. A robot teacher! Ugh!'

'My mum says it can't be worse than some *real* teachers.'

Harry raised his hand as Mrs Riley called for silence.

'Yes, Harry, what is it?'

'Do you *have* to leave at the end of term, Mrs Riley?'

Mrs Riley sighed. 'Harry,' she said patiently, 'I've already explained to you. We're moving to London at Easter. I've got to go.'

Harry nodded. He had been hoping – just hoping – that she might have changed her mind.

'In any case,' Mrs Riley said brightly, 'this robot teacher sounds *very* exciting.'

'Not to me, it doesn't,' Harry muttered.

'Don't know what *you're* moaning about,' said Norma Nicolson. 'It's *your* grandfather who's making it.'

'Yeah!' jeered Billy Bates. 'Professor Potter – the potty professor – get it?'

'That's not funny!' shouted Holly. 'He's laughing at our grandpa, Mrs Riley.'

Mrs Riley was cross. 'That's a nasty thing to say, Billy Bates. Professor Potter will be working very hard to help this class. We should all be very grateful.'

15

'You have to be very clever,' said Rashid, 'to design a robot. I saw a programme about it once.'

'Now,' said Mrs Riley briskly, 'we have a very important job to do today. We have to choose a name for your new teacher.'

'A name!' said Holly doubtfully. 'Do robots have names?'

'This one will have to,' said Mrs Riley. 'You can't go round saying, "Yes, robot. Good morning, robot." Now – can you?'

The class thought about it. Of course, Mrs Riley was right. Their robot would have to have a name.

'I want you to think about it very carefully,' said Mrs Riley. 'I will give each of you a piece of paper. When you are ready, write down your suggestion. Then fold the paper and put it in the box on my desk.'

Mrs Riley waited patiently as the children chewed their pencils and thought. Choosing a name for a robot was no easy matter. Finally, all the names were in the box and Mrs Riley gave it a good shake.

'Now, will you fetch Mr Clegg from his office, Harry? He's going to pick the name out of the box for us.'

There was silence as the headmaster came into the room. He put his hand in the box, drew out a piece of paper and unfolded it...

He glared around the classroom. 'And what bright spark,' he demanded, 'has suggested "OLD TIN CAN"?'

A giggle went round the room, quickly stifled as Mr Clegg continued to glare.

'Who was it?' he thundered.

Slowly, Billy Bates raised his hand.

'Go to my room at once, boy,' ordered the headmaster, 'and wait for me there.'

Mr Clegg waited until Billy, looking unusually pale, had left the classroom.

'I hope,' he said grimly, 'that the next suggestion will be more sensible.'

Again, he shuffled his hand around in the box,

17

took out a piece of paper and unfolded it. The class waited. He showed it to Mrs Riley. They both smiled and nodded.

'And now!' announced Mr Clegg dramatically. 'I name your new teacher...METALMISS.'

For a moment there was silence. Then 3R cheered loudly.

'And which of you thought of this name?' asked Mr Clegg.

Proudly and shyly, Rashid raised his hand.

'Well done, Rashid!' said Mr Clegg. 'A very suitable name.'

He wrote it on the blackboard. 3R stared. They muttered to themselves, trying it out.

'Metalmiss – Metalmiss.'

Yes – it looked right. It sounded right. They agreed with Mr Clegg. It was a good name for a robot teacher.

Chapter 3

The Easter holiday passed, too quickly for Harry, not quickly enough for Holly.

'Can't Grandpa let us have a look at Metalmiss?' she pleaded. 'Just a little peep.'

'No,' said Mrs Potter. 'I've told you, Holly. Not before next term. It wouldn't be fair to the other children in 3R. It would make you special.'

Mrs Potter always tried very hard to be fair. On the whole that was a good thing, but on this occasion Holly found it very tiresome.

'Well, we *are* special,' she protested. 'He's *our* grandpa. We *should* be allowed to see her.'

'That's enough, Holly,' said her mother firmly. 'I want to hear no more about it. You and Harry will just have to wait.'

Harry didn't mind. He could wait.

But, much as he might want to, he could not hold back the first day of term. New teachers were always introduced to the school at morning assembly.

Buzzing with excitement, the children crowded into the school hall. This was one new teacher they all wanted to meet. They sat on the floor, cross-legged, squashed together, facing the raised platform at the end of the hall.

All the teachers, except for the headmaster, were already sitting on the platform. There were three empty chairs.

The children nudged each other and pointed – one for Mr Clegg, one for...

Mr Jones stepped forward and raised his hand for silence. 'Stop talking now, children. And don't forget to stand up when Mr Clegg and Professor Potter come in.'

Harry turned to Holly, who was sitting behind him. 'I didn't know Grandpa was...'

20

'Sssh! Turn round!' Holly scowled at him.

'But...'

'Stand up!' hissed Holly, poking him in the back.

All around Harry the children had risen to their feet, so swiftly and silently that he hadn't even noticed. As he struggled up, he heard a quickly suppressed gasp.

There, on the platform, beside the headmaster, stood the small, white-haired figure of his grandpa. And beside him stood...METALMISS.

The children were silent – but it was a silence so charged with excitement that you could almost hear it.

The robot was made of smooth grey metal, jointed at elbows and knees. On the front of the tunic-shaped body was a large upside-down triangle, made up of rows of shiny, overlapping discs – red, yellow, green and blue. Raised above the square, grey head was a sort of cap with matching, smaller discs.

'Sit down, children,' said Mr Clegg.

Slowly, as if under a spell, the children sat down – never taking their eyes away from the strange figure on the platform.

Mr Clegg laughed, rather nervously.

'Well, Professor Potter,' he joked, 'I've never known the children to be so quiet. I don't think any new teacher has ever had *this* effect on them before.'

The children continued to stare. Nobody laughed.

Mr Clegg cleared his throat. 'I'm going to say very little this morning,' he announced. 'I shall now ask Professor Potter to introduce your new teacher.'

He sat down and Professor Potter stepped forward. Beside him, a head taller, the robot also took a step forward.

That was too much for one of the smallest juniors, sitting in the front row. With a sharp cry, she slumped sideways.

Gary Evans, sitting beside her, was not one to suffer in silence. His hand shot up. 'Miss Bird, Miss Bird,' he squeaked. 'It's Lizzie Owen, Miss. She's fainted on me.'

But, to Gary's horror, it was not his class teacher who responded.

Metalmiss took another, rather jerky, step towards the front of the platform.

'And what is the matter with Lizzie?'

There could be no doubt that the strange, metallic voice came from the robot. Gary looked around desperately. On the platform, Miss Bird rose anxiously to her feet – but sat down again at a gesture from Mr Clegg.

'What is your name?' asked Metalmiss

Gary's eyes widened in horror. 'Gary Evans,' he whispered.

'Tell me, Gary Evans, what is the matter with Lizzie?'

'I think she's fainted, Miss.' Gary looked as if he was about to do the same.

'And why has she fainted?'

Gary swallowed hard. 'I think…I think she's scared of you, Miss.'

There was a long pause. Children and teachers seemed to be holding their breath.

'And are you also scared of me, Gary Evans?'

'Yes,' whispered Gary, turning even paler, 'I am.'

Lizzie, still lying across Gary's knees, moaned softly and opened her eyes.

'Bring her to me,' commanded Metalmiss.

'But…but,' Gary protested weakly, 'she's scared of you.'

'That is why she must come. You also. Bring her here.'

Gary did not dare to disobey that commanding voice. He helped Lizzie to her feet. She seemed too dazed to understand what was happening.

The rest of the school watched in a horrified silence as the two children stumbled up the steps on to the platform.

'Three chairs, please,' ordered Metalmiss.

Three chairs were placed at the front of the platform. Shakily, the children sat down, Lizzie still clinging to Gary and looking as if she was about to faint all over again.

Metalmiss sat facing them. Her voice seemed

softer now.

'Why are you frightened, Lizzie?'

Lizzie turned to Gary but there was no help there.

'Dunno,' she muttered, staring down at her shoes.

'Look at me, Lizzie Owen.'

Fearfully, Lizzie raised her head.

As she did so, a very strange thing happened. The cold, blue-grey of the robot's eyes slowly changed to a warm, yellow glow. The two children stared.

As they stared, the glowing yellow seemed to flow over and around them. They no longer saw the robot or the other teachers or the school hall.

Instead, they felt as if they were sitting on a holiday beach, warm and relaxed, bathed in the light of a golden summer sun. Slowly, the colour returned to their cheeks. They were no longer afraid.

Only Lizzie and Gary had this feeling. The rest of the school stared in amazement as the two frightened children began to smile happily.

They were even more amazed when Lizzie put out her hand and stroked the smooth, grey steel of the robot's left arm. At the same time Metalmiss held out her right hand to Gary. He shook it gratefully.

'And now,' asked Metalmiss, standing up, 'you are both feeling better?'

'Yes, thank you,' the children chorused.

'You are no longer afraid, Lizzie Owen?'

Lizzie shook her head. Shyly she held on to the

robot's hand and looked up at the square grey head.

'I like you, Metalmiss,' she said. 'I think you're a nice teacher.'

At that, everyone laughed. A great wave of relief swept through the hall. They looked at Metalmiss, hand in hand with little Lizzie Owen and wondered why they had ever been so scared.

'Well,' said Professor Potter, 'after all that I don't think I need to introduce Metalmiss. Lizzie and Gary have done the job for me.'

'It just remains,' said Mr Clegg, 'for me to thank Professor Potter for sending Metalmiss to Pinkerton School. We will do all we can to make sure her stay with us will be a hap...'

For a moment Mr Clegg paused and looked confused. The robot's head swivelled in his direction. Hastily, he continued, 'I am sure, Metalmiss, that your stay with us will be a great success.'

Metalmiss nodded gravely. 'Thank you, Head-master. I also hope that our experiment will be successful.'

Everyone clapped.

As the children filed out of the hall, Harry stared hard at Metalmiss. As Granny had promised, it was not a scary robot. But it was still a robot and he still preferred Mrs Riley.

Chapter 4

Holly looked for her brother as 3R made its noisy way down the corridor to Room 6. He was walking along slowly, head down, by himself.

'Well?' Holly demanded eagerly. 'You didn't find Metalmiss scary, did you?'

'No,' muttered Harry.

'Didn't you like the way she cured Lizzie?'

'It was all right.'

'Well, I thought it was *fantastic*.' Holly struggled to express her feelings. 'Like...like a sort of miracle.'

Harry refused to be impressed. 'She wouldn't have needed curing if Metalmiss hadn't scared her in the first place,' he pointed out reasonably.

'It's a waste of time talking to you,' Holly said angrily. 'You've made up your mind already. You'll *never* like Metalmiss.'

With that, she ran off to join her friends.

Harry shrugged. She was probably right. It didn't matter much anyway. It certainly wouldn't matter to Metalmiss, who was a robot and had no feelings.

Suddenly Harry realised that he was the only person in the corridor. He quickened his step but as he approached Room 6 he realised that he was too late. The classroom was quiet. The door was closed.

He stared through the glass panel. 3R was

27

generally known as a noisy class, a restless class. This morning they looked like the sort of perfect class that he had seen in a TV advertisement for some kind of washing powder. Even Billy Bates was sitting up straight.

In front of them, in Mrs Riley's chair, sat Metalmiss.

Harry hated walking in late. He hated being stared at. He especially hated the thought of those steely, blue-grey eyes focusing on him.

As he hesitated, he noticed that on the wall, where the blackboard used to be, was a large screen. Like a TV screen, only much bigger. On it was drawn a plan, like the one Harry had drawn last term when his maths book said, 'Draw a plan of your classroom.'

Except that this was different. Beside the rectangle which represented Harry's table, in Rashid's place, a glowing green dot had appeared.

'Billy Bates.'

'Yes, Metalmiss.'

Another green dot, where Billy Bates sat.

Metalmiss was taking the register. As she called the names, the number of green dots multiplied rapidly. She had reached M.

If he slipped in now, perhaps she wouldn't notice.

'Norma Nicolson.'

'Yes, Metalmiss.'

This was his last chance. Harry's feet felt like lead. He couldn't move.

'Barney Phillips.'

'Yes, Metalmiss.'

'Harry Potter.'

On the screen, between the green dots of Rashid and Sally Minton, a bright red dot appeared.

Metalmiss looked up. Her eyes swept the classroom.

'Harry Potter.'

Holly raised her hand importantly. 'I'm his sister, Metalmiss. He is here. He was in the corridor.'

'There he is!' shouted Sally Minton. 'At the door.'

All heads turned towards the door. Those robot eyes were every bit as cold as Harry had imagined. They were staring straight at him.

'Come in, Harry Potter.'

Reluctantly, scarlet with embarrassment, Harry came in. He stood by the door, scowling.

'Why are you late?'

Harry gulped. 'I...I don't know. I was walking slowly, I suppose.'

'Go to your place. Do not let this happen again.'

Miserably, Harry walked to his chair and sat down.

'Holly Potter.'

'Yes, Metalmiss.'

Harry did not look up. He could imagine the smug

look on his sister's face as her green dot glowed brightly.

Metalmiss continued to take the register. Harry hated the sound of that slow, metallic voice. Lost in his own miserable thoughts, he managed to block it out completely.

'Good morning, 3R.'

Harry sat bolt upright. That was no robot. That was Mrs Riley's voice.

He looked around. 'Mrs Riley. Where's Mrs Riley?'

'On the screen, stupid,' hissed Sally. 'Video.'

Harry looked up. The plan of the classroom had disappeared and there, smiling down at him, was Mrs Riley. Beside her stood Metalmiss.

The room they were standing in looked strangely familiar. Of course! It was his grandpa's laboratory at the university.

Mrs Riley was speaking. 'Metalmiss and I have discussed your work for the term. With Professor Potter's help, we have planned it very carefully.' She smiled. 'I think you'll find that Metalmiss is no ordinary teacher. Work hard, 3R, and have a good term.'

She turned to Metalmiss. 'I've enjoyed working with you, Metalmiss. Good luck – and look after 3R.'

Metalmiss nodded. 'Thank you, Mrs Riley. I will do my best to follow your instructions.'

The screen went blank. For a few moments there was silence.

'And now,' Metalmiss announced, 'we will start on our programme for the term. Get out your red maths books. Turn to the revision exercise on page 15.'

Rashid was the first to have his work corrected. His eyes widened as Metalmiss started to mark.

'But you are not holding a pen, Metalmiss,' he blurted out. 'How do you do it?'

Metalmiss raised her head and stared at Rashid. The class waited. Rather him than me, thought Harry.

Rashid was always asking questions. Obviously, it would take more than a robot to stop him.

'I will show you, Rashid.'

Metalmiss held out her grey, metal forefinger. She turned it over. 'Do you see those three small buttons?'

Rashid examined the finger closely. He even held it in his hand. 'Yes, I can see them.'

'Press them,' commanded Metalmiss.

Rashid pressed each button in turn. The first one made a red marker appear at the tip of Metalmiss's finger; the second, black; and the third drew them both in again.

'That's clever,' said Rashid admiringly, 'like a retractable pen.'

'Yes,' nodded Metalmiss. 'My finger also has one

other function.'

She stood up and walked, rather stiffly, to the back of the classroom. Then she turned and pointed at the screen. As she moved her forefinger, the screen rapidly filled up with an exercise in multiplication.

'That was quick,' said Rashid, 'much better than the blackboard and chalk.'

'And you can watch us at the same time,' said Holly.

Sally giggled. 'Mrs Riley always did say she needed eyes at the back of her head.'

'That was a possibility,' said Metalmiss. 'But it was not considered necessary.'

Sally's eyes widened. 'She's serious,' she whispered to Harry.

'Of course she's serious, stupid,' Harry whispered back. 'She's a robot.'

'And now,' said Metalmiss, walking back to her desk. 'We will correct your other mistakes, Rashid.'

As they got on with their work, the children almost forgot who was teaching them. It began to feel like an ordinary day, with an ordinary teacher.

So normal did it feel to Billy Bates that he began using his ruler to flick paper pellets around the classroom. One of them hit Holly slap in the eye.

'Ouch!' She clapped her hand to her eye. 'That hurt!'

'Holly Potter, come here.'

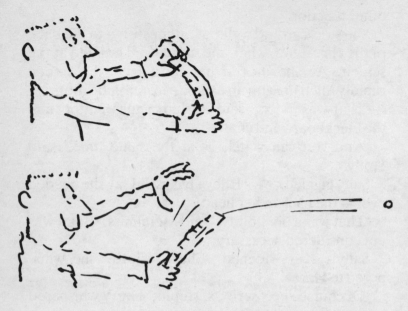

Still holding her hand over her eye, Holly stumbled to the front of the classroom.

Metalmiss was standing up. Her eyes, an icy blue, stared at Holly.

'Why are you disturbing the class?'

'I wasn't,' Holly protested. 'It was Billy Bates. He flicked a paper pellet at me. He's always doing it.'

'Come up here, Billy Bates. Is this true?'

Billy swaggered up. 'She started it, Metalmiss. I was just throwing it back.'

Holly was red with anger. 'You're lying,' she shouted. 'You started it. You know you did.'

'Didn't,' said Billy.

'Be quiet, both of you,' ordered Metalmiss. Her eyes glinted coldly.

Harry felt really sorry for his sister. He could tell that she was very close to tears.

'One of you,' said Metalmiss, 'is telling a lie.'

'He is.'

'I'm not. She is.'

Billy grinned at the class. He could fool any new teacher, never mind a silly old robot.

'Very well. Stand directly in front of me. Both of you. Look up.'

As the children looked up, a row of blue discs on the robot's cap started to revolve slowly. They began to glow – a soft blue glow which became stronger and stronger. The discs spun, faster and faster.

The class gasped with amazement as thin blue rays suddenly shot out towards the two children, encircling each head with a halo of light.

'Holly Potter, are you telling the truth?'

'Yes, Metalmiss.'

Above Holly's head, the blue halo continued to glow steadily.

'Billy Bates, are you telling the truth?'

'Yes, Metalmiss.'

There were more gasps from the class as the halo above Billy's head slowly changed from blue to red, then to deepest purple.

'You are sure, Billy Bates?'

Billy's grin had vanished. He was beginning to look very unhappy.

'Y-y-yes, Metalmiss.'

At once, the purple halo turned dark grey, then black – a thick, solid black. It looked ugly and somehow threatening as it hovered above his head.

Billy looked up fearfully.

'You are still sure, Billy Bates?'

Billy could take no more.

'I-I-I did start it,' he blubbered. 'I was lying.'

Instantly, both haloes vanished and the revolving discs were still.

'To tell a lie is a very serious matter, Billy Bates.'

'Yes, Metalmiss.' Billy stared at the floor.

'For the next three weeks you will miss your football club. You will also do extra work for me. Now you must apologise to Holly.'

'Sorry, Holly,' Billy mumbled resentfully.

'It's all right,' Holly said, smiling graciously. She wished she could keep that soft blue halo shining above her head forever.

'Return to your places. See that this does not happen again.'

Rashid's hand shot up.

'Yes, Rashid?'

'Is that a sort of lie detector, Metalmiss?'

'Yes. That is what it is. Mrs Riley considered it an essential piece of equipment.'

'She would!' muttered Billy under his breath. He hated Mrs Riley. He hated Metalmiss even more. He would get his revenge – in time.

Chapter 5

'Well, how was your new teacher?' asked their mother, as soon as the twins walked in through the door.

'Okay,' said Harry. He made straight for the sitting room and the TV.

Mrs Potter sighed. 'He doesn't like Metalmiss?'

'No,' said Holly, 'not much. But I do. I've got heaps to tell you, Mum. About Lizzie Owen and Billy Bates and the lie detector and...'

'Hold on,' laughed her mother. 'We'll have a cup of tea and you can tell me all about it. Start at the beginning.'

Harry could hear them talking and laughing in the kitchen. He turned up the TV.

Later Grandpa rang. Holly was on the phone for ages.

'She was fantastic, Grandpa. You should have seen my blue halo. I nearly died. Billy Bates was so mad when his went black. He hates Metalmiss.'

At one point there was a pause.

'Harry?...Oh, yes. He likes her too. No, he can't talk to you at the moment. He's out playing.'

Her precious blue halo would certainly have turned black at that, Harry thought. Still, he was glad. He didn't want to talk to Grandpa – not now.

Next day, Mr Jones brought a new girl up to the classroom.

'Good morning, Metalmiss,' he said, slowly and clearly. 'This is Maria Bellini. She is Italian. She speaks very little English.'

From the way he spoke, Harry could tell that Mr Jones felt uncomfortable about talking to a robot.

Maria clutched Mr Jones's hand tightly as she stared at Metalmiss.

Poor girl, thought Harry. New town, new language, new school – *and* a robot teacher. No wonder she looked scared.

'Good morning, Maria,' said Metalmiss. 'Mrs Riley has told me about you.'

At the sound of the strange voice, Maria moved closer to Mr Jones.

On the robot's tunic a row of shiny green discs began to revolve slowly. Maria's eyes widened and she clutched Mr Jones's hand even more tightly.

Metalmiss began to speak.

The children stared at each other. She was talking nonsense. They couldn't understand a word.

But Maria could. Her mouth open in disbelief, she stared at Metalmiss. Mr Jones was looking more and more worried. Were all his fears about robots to be confirmed?

Gradually, as she listened, Maria loosened her grip on Mr Jones's hand. She began to smile happily.

Then she began to chatter – on and on as if she would never stop.

Mr Jones looked in astonishment from Metalmiss to Maria and back again. His serious face softened into a smile.

Metalmiss said something to Maria, who nodded and turned to Mr Jones.

'Thank you, Mr Jones,' she said, slowly and carefully. 'I happy now. I talk to teacher.'

'Yes, I can see you do,' said Mr Jones. 'Amazing – quite amazing.'

Still looking rather dazed, he thanked Metalmiss and hurried off to join his own class.

Rashid raised his hand excitedly. 'Can you speak *any* language, Metalmiss?'

'Only if I am programmed to do so.'

'Can you speak *my* language?'

'Yes, Rashid. But I do not need to. Your English is excellent. Soon Maria will also speak good English.'

Metalmiss talked to Maria while the rest of the class answered questions from their Language Workcards. They were allowed to discuss these questions as long as they did so quietly.

Quiet discussion was not 3R's strong point. The classroom was getting noisier. Norma Nicolson and her friend Tracey were not even talking about the workcards. They were having a heated argument about their favourite TV programme.

Suddenly there was a loud buzzing noise, like an alarm clock only much louder. The children stopped talking. Metalmiss stood up. They noticed that near the top of her cap some red discs were glowing brightly.

'This noise level is not acceptable, 3R. Tracey and Norma, come up here.'

The two girls looked at each other in surprise.

'Tracey, touch the red disc on the front of my cap.'

As soon as Tracey touched it, she jumped back in amazement. There was her own voice, loud and clear.

'Belinda *is* married to Gary, Norma.'

Then Norma's voice. 'No, she isn't, Tracey. She *was* married to Gary. Now she's married to Pete.'

The class laughed loudly. Most of the children knew all about the TV programme that was being discussed. Holly and Harry always felt cross because they weren't allowed to watch it.

Tracey's voice again. 'No, stupid. Mandy is married to Pete. Belinda is married to Gary.'

Harry began to think that his mother was probably right about the programme. It all sounded very boring. Holly would probably like it though.

'I am programmed with all the questions on your workcards. I do not recall a question about Belinda and Gary and Mandy and Pete. Is there such a question?'

At this the class laughed even more loudly. Not Tracey and Norma.

'No, Metalmiss,' they whispered.

'In future you are to discuss only the questions on your card. Is that clear?'

'Yes, Metalmiss.'

The robot's icy gaze swept the classroom.

'This noise level is still not acceptable, 3R. Work quietly.' The red discs in the robot's cap continued to glow until the laughter had died away completely.

None of them laughed at what happened that afternoon.

'Oh, no,' groaned Sally as a loud continuous ringing sounded throughout the school, 'fire drill again. *Boring.*'

'Silence!' ordered Metalmiss. 'Into line. Take your usual route to the playground. Do not run.'

As they left the classroom, there was a faint but unmistakable smell of burning. Holly and Harry looked at each other. This was no practice. This was the real thing.

In the playground the classes lined up in silence. Registers were taken. The teachers looked tense and worried.

Mr Clegg addressed the children. 'At the moment the fire is confined to the kitchen area. The fire brigade should be here before it spreads any further.

We have to be sure that…'

Mr Roberts, white faced, rushed up to the headmaster. 'Katie Watson, Mr Clegg. Katie Watson's missing. She should have been back from her piano lesson.'

Mr Clegg also went pale.

Katie Watson's Missing

'Has anyone seen Katie Watson?' he shouted. 'From Mr Roberts's class.'

No one had seen her.

They could see the kitchen. It was full of smoke and the smell of burning was getting stronger. As they watched, flames began to lick at the windows.

'Oh, no!' moaned Mr Roberts. 'She could be anywhere. I'm going to look.'

'Wait!' Metalmiss stepped forward. 'I will find out where she is.'

'I haven't time...'

Mr Roberts stopped abruptly and stared at Metalmiss.

From her eyes two strong beams of light shot out, like searchlights. For a few seconds they swept the building. Children and teachers watched in silence.

The searching stopped. Metalmiss turned to Mr Roberts. 'She is upstairs, at the back of the building, in the library,' she announced. 'It is safe to go there.'

As Mr Roberts ran off, the fire brigade arrived. The fire, although fierce, had not spread much further. It was soon contained and overcome.

Rashid was scarcely able to contain his excitement. 'X-ray eyes. That's what she's got, Harry. Just like that film about...'

At this point Mr Roberts arrived back with a very frightened Katie. She was trembling all over and sobbing loudly.

Mr Roberts explained that she had slipped into the library on the way back from her music lesson. When she heard the fire bell she thought it was a practice and hadn't bothered to return to the classroom.

'That was very silly of you, Katie,' scolded Mr Clegg. 'And *very* dangerous. Do you realise that you could have been killed?'

'Yes, Mr Clegg,' sobbed Katie.

'I think you've learnt your lesson, Katie,' said Mr Clegg more gently. 'We'll say no more about it.'

He turned to the rest of the school.

'I think we have *all* learnt a valuable lesson this afternoon. We are very grateful to Metalmiss for helping us to find Katie so quickly.'

Mr Roberts stepped forward. 'Three cheers for Metalmiss,' he shouted. 'Hip! Hip!'

As the children cheered, Miss Bird turned to Metalmiss.

'I knew you would be a success, Metalmiss,' she beamed. 'That was amazing.'

'It is not amazing,' said Metalmiss. 'It is what I am programmed to do.'

Chapter 6

Mr Clegg had just entered his office next morning when Miss Vickers, the school secretary, came rushing in.

'It's Mr Robertson on the phone, Mr Clegg, from the Education Office. He sounds very upset.'

'Big fuss about nothing, I expect, as usual,' muttered Mr Clegg as he took off his coat.

But this time there *was* something to fuss about.

'Inspection!' exclaimed Mr Clegg. 'Today!'

Mr Robertson explained that inspectors from Head Office in London were visiting various schools around the country. Schools were not to be told until the day of the visit. He had just been informed that a Mr Grimshaw was to spend the day at Pinkerton Primary.

'Not Grouchy Grimshaw!' gasped Mr Clegg. 'I've heard about him!'

'I know,' groaned Mr Robertson. 'Couldn't be

47

worse. The thing is that I haven't got round to telling Head Office about your robot teacher. Grimshaw mustn't see it or we'll both be in deep trouble.'

'And how am I supposed to manage that?' demanded Mr Clegg.

'Can't help you there, I'm afraid. But I'm sure you'll think of something. JUST DON'T LET GRIMSHAW NEAR THE ROBOT.'

With that, Mr Robertson rang off.

'Thanks a lot,' Mr Clegg muttered bitterly as he put down the phone.

All the teachers, except Metalmiss, were in the staffroom. Most of them had heard of Mr Grimshaw.

'Nastiest inspector in the country,' said Mr Jones. 'Everyone hates him. Never been known to give a good report.'

'You won't keep *him* away from Metalmiss,' said Mr Roberts. 'Not Grouchy Grimshaw.'

'And who,' asked a clear metallic voice, 'is Grouchy Grimshaw?'

Metalmiss had entered the staffroom.

'Just a silly little person,' said Miss Bird hastily. 'Nobody important.'

'I thought there might be a problem,' said Metalmiss. 'The registration bell is late.'

'Goodness, so it is!' exclaimed Mr Jones, looking at his watch. 'To your classrooms, everyone!'

Mr Clegg had no sooner hurried back to his office than there was a loud knock on the door. Without waiting for any response, a fat, bad-tempered looking man marched into the room.

'Was that the registration bell?' he demanded,

glaring at Mr Clegg through thick round spectacles. 'Bit late, isn't it? Sign of a sloppy school. I'm Grimshaw. I hate sloppy schools.'

'Would you like some coffee, Mr Grimshaw?' Miss Vickers asked hastily.

'While we discuss your plans for the day,' added Mr Clegg.

'No coffee,' barked Mr Grimshaw. 'Waste of time. As for my plans, Mr Clegg, they're very simple. I just wander about the school and pop into various classrooms. That should tell me all I want to know.'

'Yes,' sighed Mr Clegg under his breath. 'I'm afraid it might.'

'What did you say?'

'I said, "I'm sure you're right", Mr Grimshaw.'

Mr Clegg watched helplessly as the school inspector marched off. Room 6 was at the far end of the corridor.

Miss Bird spotted Mr Grimshaw peering through the glass panel in her classroom door. She flung the door wide open.

'You must be Mr Grimshaw,' she gushed. 'Do come in.'

Mr Grimshaw was so startled that he came in at once.

The children in Miss Bird's class were working in groups, pouring water into various containers.

'Now children, show our visitor how carefully you

can estimate and measure in litres and millilitres.'

Instead of walking around and talking to the children, Mr Grimshaw took a chair and placed it at the back of the room. There he sat, scowling at the class, and occasionally writing in a small, black notebook.

'Mary, be careful! That jug's too full!'

Mary, on her way to the sink, swivelled round sharply.

'It's all right, Miss Bird. I can man...aaagh!'

'You stupid girl!' The inspector sprang to his feet, dripping wet and purple with rage. 'Just look what you've done!'

Mary burst into tears and Miss Bird rushed over to comfort her.

'I'm sorry, Mr Grimshaw. But it was an accident. Mary tripped over your foot. She didn't mean...'

'She's a stupid girl!' bellowed Mr Grimshaw as he stormed damply out of the room. 'And you, Miss Bird, are a sloppy teacher. Head Office will hear about this.'

'Oh, dear!' sighed Miss Bird. Instead of helping, she had made matters much worse. What would Mr Clegg say?

Mr Clegg, confronted by a drenched and furious school inspector, was allowed to say very little. He felt distinctly relieved when Miss Vickers bounced into the room, brandishing a bright pink tracksuit.

'Belongs to Mrs Clarke, our caretaker's wife.'
Miss Vickers examined Mr Grimshaw critically.
'She's rather a large lady, so it should fit.'

'I can't wear *that*!' Mr Grimshaw protested
fiercely. 'School inspectors don't wear pink track-
suits!'

'I'm afraid you've got no choice,' Miss Vickers said
briskly. 'Otherwise you'll catch your death of cold.
You can change in my office and I'll get your suit
dried straight away.'

Mr Grimshaw had already begun to shiver and
sneeze violently.

'Oh, all right,' he snarled, grabbing the tracksuit
and vanishing into the inner office.

'Perhaps,' said Miss Vickers hopefully, 'he won't
want to do his inspecting in a pink tracksuit.'

'It would take more than that to stop *him*,' said Mr
Clegg gloomily.

The inspector emerged, scowling unhappily.

'Ooh, Mr Grimshaw!' exclaimed Miss Vickers.
'It's a perfect fit. Quite suits him, doesn't it, Mr
Clegg?'

Mr Clegg was just thinking that the school
inspector closely resembled a large, pink and very
cross looking hippopotamus.

'Doesn't it suit him, Mr Clegg?'

Mr Clegg blinked. 'Er…yes…very…'

'Don't be silly,' snapped Mr Grimshaw. 'I look

quite ridiculous. But it won't stop me doing my job. You can be sure of that, Mr Clegg. This time I'm starting at the other end of the corridor.'

'Oh, no!' groaned Mr Clegg as the inspector trundled off. 'He's heading straight for Room 6. There's no stopping him this time.'

But Mr Jones, lurking outside Room 5, was determined to try.

'Ah, Mr Grimshaw!' he exclaimed, taking the inspector by the arm and trying to steer him away from Room 6. 'Sorry to hear about your little accident. I'm Jones, Deputy Head. I've been waiting to show you our development plans for the school. I think you'll find them very exciting, very...'

'No, Mr Jones,' barked Mr Grimshaw, jerking his arm away. 'I do not want to see your boring plans. I want to see teachers – TEACHERS, MR JONES!'

'But...'

'What is this noise? You are disturbing my class.'

Mr Grimshaw turned pale and shrank back against the wall as Metalmiss approached.

'Wha-wha-what's that?' he gasped.

Metalmiss gave him a cold stare.

'I am a robot teacher. Who are you?'

'Gr-Gr-Grimshaw.'

'Grimshaw?' Metalmiss paused. Her head swivelled towards Mr Jones. 'Is this the Grouchy Grimshaw who was mentioned in the staffroom,

Mr Jones?'

'Well...yes...I mean...no...' stuttered Mr Jones helplessly as the school inspector glared at him.

'Is he to join my class?'

'Yes, in a way, but he's a...'

'Very well. Come into my classroom, Grouchy. And no more shouting.'

3R watched in amazement as a fat, bespectacled man in a pink tracksuit was led into the room.

'We have a new pupil this afternoon, children. Grouchy Grimshaw.'

A giggle went round the classroom but was soon stopped by the robot's steely gaze.

'For the moment, Grouchy, you can sit there, in Rashid's place. He is away today.'

Mr Grimshaw sat down beside Harry.

'Now Grouchy,' said Metalmiss, 'we have just completed some experiments with water. I will check that you are familiar with these. Harry, will you place the container of water in front of our new pupil.'

'Not water again!' groaned Mr Grimshaw.

'Pupils in 3R do not complain about their lessons, Grouchy. That is something you must learn. Now – when does water become solid?'

'When it freezes, of course,' said Mr Grimshaw scornfully.

'Good. Now I will make this water freeze.'

'I don't think you'll do that in a hurry,' laughed Mr

Grimshaw, stirring the water with his finger. He wondered why he had ever felt frightened of this silly robot.

'Take your finger out,' hissed Harry.

'Remove your finger from the water, Grouchy,' ordered Metalmiss.

'Why?' Mr Grimshaw stirred more wildly. 'Why should I?'

Metalmiss pointed at the water. The grey steel of her finger slowly changed to a brilliant, dazzling blue.

Harry grabbed Mr Grimshaw's hand and pulled it clear, just in time.

The water in the container was now a solid block of ice. Mr Grimshaw turned pale as he stared from his finger to the ice and back again.

'Is ice heavier or lighter than water, Grouchy?'

'Heavier,' said Mr Grimshaw faintly. He was still recovering from his chilling experience.

Holly raised her hand. 'It's lighter, Metalmiss, like an iceberg.'

'Good, Holly. That is correct.'

Harry began to feel sorry for Mr Grimshaw.

Metalmiss broke off a chunk of ice and they watched it float in a glass of water.

'I meant lighter,' growled Mr Grimshaw.

'Then you must say what you mean, Grouchy. But do not worry. You will soon catch up with the other children in 3R.'

This was too much for Mr Grimshaw. He leapt to his feet.

'I am not a child!' he shouted. 'I will not be treated like a child!'

'Sit down at once, Grouchy.'

The robot's eyes were as cold as the ice in the glass. Mr Grimshaw sat down.

'You say that you are not a child. You are not a teacher. You are not a parent. What are you?'

'I am a School Inspector.'

'An inspector. I have not been programmed for that. 'Please wait.'

Metalmiss walked to the back of the room. Then she turned, pressed a small red button on the side of her left wrist, and pointed her left forefinger at the screen. Words beginning with 'I' slid rapidly across the screen and then halted.

'Here it is... "inspect"... "inspector"... "one who inspects; official employed to supervise a service and make reports".'

'That's it!' cried Mr Grimshaw triumphantly. 'I inspect schools and write reports. And what a report I'm going to write about this school!'

Metalmiss walked slowly back to the front of the classroom, turned round and stared at him.

'Will your report be a good one, Inspector?'

Mr Grimshaw's smile of triumph faded as his eyes

met the robot's steely gaze.

'Er...yes,' he mumbled.

On the robot's cap a row of blue discs began to revolve, slowly at first, then faster. The children nudged each other. They knew what was coming.

Even so, they gasped as the blue rays suddenly shot out and formed a halo above Mr Grimshaw's head.

'You are sure, Inspector?'

'Yes.'

The halo changed to purple, to grey, to black.

'It's a lie detector,' Harry whispered.

'You are still sure that it will be a good report?'

'No!' screamed Mr Grimshaw, knocking his chair over as he jumped to his feet. 'I am going to write a VERY BAD REPORT!'

The halo disappeared.

'In fact,' Mr Grimshaw continued viciously, 'it will be the worst report that I have ever written. Sloppy school – sloppy teachers – and just wait until I tell Head Office about *you*, Metalmiss!'

'Sit down,' Metalmiss commanded.

For a moment Mr Grimshaw stared back defiantly. Then he shrugged, picked up his chair and sat down. He could wait.

Metalmiss turned to the class.

'And now, 3R, before you go to your music lesson I will read some more of our story.'

The story was about sailing ships and islands full of buried treasure. The robot's voice seemed softer, less metallic. On her tunic discs spun, glowed, changed colour. The blue of the sea rippled softly over the ceiling and walls of the classroom. Shapes of tall palm trees swayed in a gentle breeze and the treasure shone in pools of gold, ruby red and emerald green.

As he listened, Mr Grimshaw removed his glasses and began to breathe deeply. His face, usually so bad-tempered, grew softer, almost dreamy. He sat in a blur of colour, listening to the slow, clear voice. It *was* like a dream, he thought, the sort of dream that you want to go on for ever and ever. For the first time in many years he felt young and happy. No school had ever done *that* for him before.

The story ended. Quietly, the children went off to their music lesson. Mr Grimshaw sat on.

'Did you like our story, Inspector?'

Mr Grimshaw blinked, fumbled for his glasses and put them on. He beamed at Metalmiss.

'It was wonderful – just wonderful. I can't find words to describe it.'

'But you will find words for your report, Inspector?'

'Yes, but now I will have to find new words, Metalmiss. It will be my first good report – a *very* good report.'

'And will you mention a robot teacher?'

'Not a robot – just a very special kind of teacher.'

Mr Grimshaw stood up and shook hands. 'I have to go now, Metalmiss. Goodbye – and thank you.'

'Goodbye, Inspector.'

'I'm very sorry, Mr Grimshaw,' Mr Clegg began nervously as the school inspector entered his office, 'we meant to tell you about...'

'About your special teacher,' interrupted Mr Grimshaw, beaming widely. 'I must congratulate you, Mr Clegg – marvellous teachers – marvellous school. Do apologise to Miss Bird for me. Shouldn't have been angry. Not her fault at all.'

'But-but...' stuttered Mr Clegg.

'Ah!' exclaimed Mr Grimshaw. 'I see that my suit is dry already. I'll get changed at once and be on my way.'

'What...what about the other teachers?'

'No need to see them. I've seen enough – more than enough. I'll send you a copy of my report, Mr Clegg.'

A few days later there was a phone call.

'For you, Mr Clegg,' said Miss Vickers, smiling. 'Education Office.'

It was Mr Robertson.

'I've got Grimshaw's report here, Mr Clegg. He

thinks your school is wonderful. I can't believe it. He's never written a report like that before.'

'I know,' said Mr Clegg. 'I've got a copy.'

'No mention of a robot either. How did you manage it?'

'Oh, we do our best,' said Mr Clegg airily, winking at Miss Vickers. 'But I do agree with Mr Grimshaw. There *is* something special about Pinkerton Primary.'

Chapter 7

'We're off to the zoo, zoo, zoo,' Holly sang tunelessly as she came down to breakfast. 'How about you, you, you?'

'Not me, thank goodness,' said her father. 'Eat your cereal.'

It was the day for 3R's outing. They were going to Whitmore Zoo.

'I do hope Metalmiss can cope,' said Mrs Potter anxiously.

''Course she can,' said Holly. 'It – is – what – she – is – programmed – to – do.'

Harry couldn't help giggling. Holly sounded just like a robot.

'Don't worry, Mum,' Holly added. 'Mr Jones and Mr Roberts are coming along as well.'

'I think *all* teachers need nerves of steel for this sort of occasion,' said Mr Potter. 'I don't know how they stand it.'

When the twins got to school they found the whole class in a state of excitement, comparing picnics and squabbling over partners for the bus. Rashid was Harry's partner. Holly chose Sally Minton.

They all calmed down when Metalmiss came into the room. She took the register.

'Get into line with your partners, 3R. The bus has arrived.'

At the bus, Mr Jones and Mr Roberts were waiting for them. Chattering excitedly, the children piled on.

They were chattering so much that they scarcely noticed the journey. In no time at all, they had arrived at Whitmore Zoo.

'That was quick,' said Sally. 'Seems to take much longer by car.'

At the zoo, they were divided into three groups of ten. Harry and Holly and their partners were all with Metalmiss.

'It's not fair,' muttered Harry. 'I wanted to be in Mr Jones's group.'

'Not me,' said Rashid. 'Metalmiss is much more interesting.'

The zoo had provided a guide for each group. Their guide was called Mr Lyon.

'Lyon with "y",' he explained as they all laughed. 'Good name for a zoo guide, don't you think?'

Metalmiss did not laugh. Mr Lyon looked at her uneasily.

First he took them to the monkeys. There were a lot of monkeys, swinging about, chattering and screaming.

'I bet your teacher thinks they sound just like you lot,' he joked.

'No,' said Metalmiss, giving him an icy stare. 'I do not think so. They sound like monkeys. These children are not monkeys.'

Mr Lyon cleared his throat nervously. 'No...of course not...only joking,' he stuttered. 'Not monkeys...children...yes, quite.'

'He will soon learn,' whispered Rashid, 'that robots do not make jokes.'

'What are those called, Mr Lyon?' asked Holly, pointing to four brown haired, sharp eyed little monkeys. Each one had a black cap of hair coming to a point on its forehead.

'Those,' Mr Lyon explained gratefully, 'are Capuchin Monkeys. They come from South America.'

One bright-eyed Capuchin was sitting on a branch, staring fixedly at Metalmiss.

'I am sure it knows,' said Rashid excitedly, 'that she is not human.'

Suddenly the little monkey bared its teeth and began to make a shrill, chattering noise. He jumped up and down frantically, his eyes still fixed on Metalmiss.

Gradually all the monkeys, in all the cages, fell silent. They crouched on branches or on the ground, absolutely still, their sharp, bright eyes staring at Metalmiss.

'Very strange,' frowned Mr Lyon. 'I've never seen them behave like this before.'

'I'm scared,' said Holly, moving closer to Sally. 'It's really creepy.'

'I think,' said Mr Lyon, 'that we will move on to the Spider Monkeys. They also come from South America. They communicate by...'

Before he could say any more, some of the Spider Monkeys decided to communicate – *very* loudly. Some barked sharply while others made deep growling noises.

Quickly Mr Lyon moved on to the next cage. 'These monkeys,' he said desperately, 'are called Howler Monkeys because...'

He did not have to explain any further as the Howler Monkeys began to howl. The children found it hard to believe that a few monkeys could make so much noise.

'I think,' yelled Mr Lyon, as the noise began to die down, 'that we will leave the monkeys and move on to...'

He stopped abruptly as Metalmiss stepped forward. He took a sharp step backwards and crashed into the wire mesh of the cage. The monkeys

started to howl again, even more loudly. Trapped between Metalmiss and the Howlers, poor Mr Lyon looked quite sick.

'Do not be afraid, Mr Lyon,' said Metalmiss. 'I am only a teacher.'

Mr Lyon was not convinced.

'Could you all move back, please,' said Metalmiss. The children moved back.

After a moment's hesitation, so did Mr Lyon.

As Metalmiss approached the cages, the monkeys fell silent again. They shrank back fearfully, clutching each other for comfort.

Metalmiss did not speak. The monkeys stared, as if hypnotised, at the robot's cold, blue eyes.

As they stared, the blue slowly changed to a warm, glowing yellow.

'Look,' whispered Sally. 'It's like when she cured Lizzie Owen.'

The golden glow seemed to pour into all the cages, filling them with warmth and light.

Older monkeys, from South America and Africa, felt as if they were back there again – swinging through the forests, wild and free. Youngsters, born in the zoo, felt the heat of a sun that they had never known.

Happily, they began to chatter and leap and swing. When the golden light vanished, they continued to play – no longer afraid of this strange new creature.

'And now,' said Metalmiss, turning round, 'I think we should leave the monkeys.'

'Yes,' said Mr Lyon, looking dazed, 'I think we should.'

His face brightened as he consulted his watch. 'I'm afraid we're running rather late. It will have to be a quick tour of the other animals.'

He allowed them a brief look at the elephants and the giraffes.

'Bet he makes a joke about his name when we come to the lions,' said Harry.

But he didn't. They were whisked past the big cats in no time at all. Mr Lyon with a 'y' was not in the mood for jokes.

'You've missed the gorillas, Mr Lyon,' protested Billy Bates, as they were hustled along. 'They're over there.'

Mr Lyon looked at him with dislike. 'I hadn't forgotten,' he said sharply, 'I was just coming to them.'

The gorilla enclosure was large and grassy. It was surrounded by a deep ditch and a high wall. Four gorillas were sitting in a group. A huge, top heavy male was pacing about on all fours, looking very fierce.

'Ugh!' exclaimed Holly. 'I wouldn't like to meet one of those.'

'That,' said Mr Lyon, 'is a silverbacked male. In

spite of their appearance, gorillas are quiet and gentle creatures. They...'

He was interrupted by a sharp scream.

'Oh, no!' gasped Holly.

A boy from another school had climbed on to the wall and jerked backwards as a teacher grabbed at him. They watched in horror as he fell. At the bottom of the ditch, a long way down, he lay still.

'Look!' Sally pointed.

The huge Silverback had heard the scream and seen the child fall. He gave a sharp grunt and stopped pacing about. For a few moments he stood still. Then he roared – a loud and terrifying roar.

'*That* doesn't sound very gentle,' gasped Sally, clutching at Holly.

'I wish some help would come,' said Holly, almost crying.

'Help will be here in a few moments,' said Mr Lyon. 'Don't worry. The gorilla won't harm him.'

'Wish I was so sure,' muttered Harry, as the Silverback started to make strange hooting noises. The hoots became louder and louder until they merged into another ear splitting, screaming roar.

'He's just nervous,' said Mr Lyon. 'Nothing to worry about.'

Suddenly the huge gorilla stood upright.

As the crowd held its breath, he began to beat on his chest with his hands. In the silence, the hollow sound was loud and clear.

'Me Tarzan,' intoned Billy Bates. 'Me tough.'

Nobody laughed.

Suddenly the chest beating stopped and the gorilla dropped on to all fours again. Slowly, it began to lumber towards the spot where the child had fallen.

'Metalmiss!' cried Rashid. 'She will help.'

'Oh, no!' groaned Mr Lyon. 'Not again.'

Rashid grabbed Metalmiss by the arm and pulled her to the spot where the child had fallen over. Mr Lyon and the rest of the group followed.

'This is our teacher,' announced Rashid. 'She will rescue him.'

The teachers from the other school looked doubtfully at Metalmiss. But they did not protest. They were ready to try anything. The boy's name, they said, was Michael.

By now the gorilla had reached the edge of the bank. It began to edge its way down the grassy slope towards the child. At the bottom of the ditch Michael still lay, unmoving.

Metalmiss reached over the wall.

'It's no good,' Michael's teacher moaned. 'She'll never reach him.'

'You wait,' said Rashid. 'Something will happen.'

And it did.

At the robot's elbows the metal joints began to glow, orange and then red. Slowly, her arms grew longer and longer.

The huge animal was now crouching beside Michael. It bent forward...

'Hey! That's my ball. Give it back.'

Rashid had seized a child's ball and thrown it at the bank, directly behind the gorilla. It looked round sharply.

As it did so, the robot's hands slid gently under Michael's back. Then, as the long arms smoothly retracted, he was lifted swiftly into the air and up over the wall.

When the gorilla turned back, the child had vanished. It gave a deep grunt of surprise and anger. For some time it lumbered about on all fours, puzzled, shaking its head from side to side. Then, slowly, it made its way back up the grassy slope.

Michael had been rushed to hospital, suffering from concussion and a broken leg. He would be all right.

Everyone crowded around Metalmiss.

'You are lucky,' a strange child said to Rashid. 'Wish we had a robot teacher.'

'I don't know how to thank you,' Michael's teacher kept saying to Metalmiss.

'There is no need,' said Metalmiss. 'It is what I am programmed to do.'

She looked around. 'Where is Mr Lyon, children? We must thank him for being our guide.'

But Mr Lyon with a 'y' was not to be found. He had had more than enough for one day.

Soon it was time to go home. Mr Roberts counted them on to the bus.

'Well,' he commented. 'You've had quite a day, children. Have you enjoyed it?'

'Yes, Mr Roberts,' they chorused.

They were unusually quiet on the way home. As Mr Roberts said, they had had quite a day. It had been – different.

Chapter 8

Harry was almost home when he realised that he'd left his anorak in the classroom.

'You're always forgetting things,' Holly said crossly. 'I'm not going back with you. You can fetch it yourself.'

'Nobody asked you to,' said Harry. 'But you can take my bag and tell Mum where I am.'

'All right,' said Holly grudgingly, 'but don't be long.'

'Bet you left it on the bus, anyway,' she called after him.

Had he? Harry worried about that as he ran down the street. Mum would kill him.

He reached the school, ran up the stairs and panted into the classroom. There, on the back of his chair, was the blue anorak.

As he picked it up he heard voices in the corridor.

'You're right there, my lad. It's a big responsibility. After school, I'm in sole charge of her.'

It was Mr Clarke, the caretaker.

'What happens then, Mr Clarke? What do you do with her?'

That was Billy Bates. What was he doing here? Had he forgotten something as well?

'You're really interested, aren't you, Billy?'

'Oh yeah, Mr Clarke. I'm dead keen on robots.'

Robots! Harry frowned. They must be talking about Metalmiss.

''Course I had to spend a week up at the university with Professor Potter,' Mr Clarke was boasting. 'You have to be properly trained to look after robots, you know.'

'Can't be easy, Mr Clarke. What sort of things do you have to do?'

'Come along and I'll show you, Billy. She stays in my room, of course. After school, I take out the control box and recharge...'

74

The voices faded away down the corridor. Harry stood still, thinking. Since when had Billy Bates been so interested in robots? What was he up to?

'Well, are you going to be here all day, young man?'

Mrs Green, the cleaning lady, had come into the room.

'I forgot my anorak. I'm just going.'

'And how do you like your new teacher, then?'

'She's okay.'

'Well, I'll say this for her. She's a lot cleaner and tidier than *some* teachers I could mention.'

'Yes,' said Harry. 'She always makes us tidy up properly.'

'All the same,' said Mrs Green with a shudder. 'A robot! Gives me the creeps just to think about it. Bet you'd rather have a normal teacher, wouldn't you?'

'Yes,' said Harry, 'I would.'

'Better run along now, my lad. Your mum'll be wondering where you are.'

Harry walked home slowly. Billy Bates hated Metalmiss. Why was he suddenly so keen on robots?

'What took you so long, Harry?' Mrs Potter scolded. 'I was getting really worried about you.'

'I told him to hurry up, Mum,' Holly said in her goody goody voice.

Harry pulled a face. He certainly wasn't going to

tell *her* about Billy Bates.

Anyway, what did he care about Metalmiss? Why should he care if anything happened to her? He hadn't even wanted her in the first place.

All the same, he felt strangely relieved to see Metalmiss at her desk next morning. He looked at Billy Bates. Billy didn't look any different either.

Metalmiss took the register as usual. She stood up.

'We will now go out to the playground, children. You will each throw a beanbag and measure the length of your throw in metres. Rashid and Harry, will you please fetch the trundle wheels from the maths cupboard? I will carry the sack of beanbags.'

In the playground, the children threw the beanbags, guessed the length of their throw and measured with the trundle wheels. They wrote down the results in their notebooks.

Harry enjoyed this sort of thing. It was much more fun than sitting in the classroom, doing sums. Unfortunately, it was also the sort of thing that didn't always work with 3R. This time was no different.

'You never threw ten metres, Norma Nicolson. You're cheating.'

'I am not, Sally Minton. Just because yours was a titchy little... ouch!'

A beanbag, travelling at great speed, had smacked into Norma's shoulder.

'Metalmiss!' she yelled. 'Someone's throwing... ow!' Another beanbag caught her on the knee. She hopped around frantically. 'That hurt! Metalmiss! Help!'

She ducked as more beanbags came whizzing towards her.

The other children had stopped measuring and were staring in disbelief.

'I don't believe it,' gasped Holly. 'It's Metalmiss. She's throwing them.'

Metalmiss was standing beside a pile of beanbags. Her arms were spinning like windmills as she sent them flying.

'Watch out!' screamed Sally, as a beanbag narrowly missed her head. They were now hurtling around the playground in all directions.

The children dropped their trundle wheels and ran and ducked and dodged. Harry was pleased to see Billy Bates get a beanbag smack on the back of his neck. Somehow he was responsible for this. Harry was sure of it.

Then, suddenly, Metalmiss stopped and stood still. The children flopped to the ground, exhausted.

'Collect all trundle wheels and beanbags. That is the end of our maths lesson.'

'Maths lesson!' gasped Sally, as they trooped back into school. 'Some maths lesson!'

'I'm really worried,' said Holly. 'Something's very

wrong. That's not normal.'

'Normal for a potty old robot,' jeered Billy Bates, as he walked past them.

'You shut up, Billy Bates,' scowled Holly. 'Nobody asked for your opinion.'

When they got back to the classroom, it was as if nothing at all unusual had happened. Slowly and clearly, Metalmiss explained what they had to do. Then the children got on with their work – very quietly. Harry breathed a sigh of relief. Whatever had happened, that seemed to be the end of it. Perhaps he was wrong about Billy Bates.

In the afternoon it was 3R's turn to use the art room. They were finishing off some collage pictures. Harry had painted a blue green sea in the background and now he was sticking on bits of material to make a ship. He wasn't very good at art but it was beginning to look quite colourful. He hoped people would know it was a ship.

Holly was doing a lady in a beautiful ball gown. Every year she did a lady in a beautiful ball gown. Her bedroom wall was covered with them. So far, this one looked just as boring as all the others.

'Harry,' whispered Rashid, who was making a very fat fish out of shiny paper, 'look at Metalmiss.'

Harry looked.

'Oh, no!' he groaned. 'Not again!'

Metalmiss had grabbed the biggest brush she could

find in the art room cupboard. They watched, horrified, as she began to decorate the classroom wall with thick lines of bright pink paint.

By now the other children had seen what was happening. Work on the collages came to a halt. Harry looked at Billy Bates. He was smiling. It was not a nice smile.

'Her programming has gone very wrong,' said Rashid, frowning. 'I do not understand.'

'I do,' said Harry grimly.

Metalmiss was now adding large circular shapes, in vivid yellow. Nobody knew what to do. Some of the children were giggling nervously.

Billy Bates climbed on to one of the tables. He pretended to have a microphone in his hand.

'Roll up, folks!' he yelled. 'Roll up for the exhibition of modern art. Art by robots – art as you have never seen it before!'

At that, the children laughed and cheered and clapped. Harry knew 3R. They were about to become *very* noisy and *very* silly.

'Can't we *do* something?' Holly was almost crying.

'I don't think so,' said Harry. 'She's out of control.'

But there was something he could do. He whispered to Holly and Rashid and slipped quietly out of the room. Nobody saw him go.

He ran all the way to Mr Clegg's office and burst in

without even knocking.

'What on earth...?' Mr Clegg looked very angry.

'Please Mr Clegg,' Harry panted. 'Ring Grandpa – Metalmiss – Billy Bates – out of control.'

Mr Clegg peered at him. 'Ah, yes, Professor Potter's grandson. Now calm down and tell me all about it.'

Harry told him.

'It's not like telling tales, is it, Mr Clegg?' he asked anxiously.

'Oh, no,' said Mr Clegg, looking very angry. 'It's much too important for that. You go back to the art room and I'll come along as soon as I've phoned your grandfather.'

Harry could hear 3R long before he reached them. They were screaming with laughter. Billy Bates was still in full swing. Harry slipped in, unnoticed.

'What has she been doing?' he asked, looking at the mess on the wall.

'She's put masses of that strong paste on top of the paint,' Holly said miserably. 'She's sticking on anything she can find in the cupboard.'

As she spoke, Metalmiss carried a box of macaroni from the cupboard to the wall. Handful by handful, she squashed it into the paste.

'That belongs to 4B,' Rashid groaned. 'They were going to do pictures with pasta.'

The wall was now plastered with oddments of material, coloured paper, milk bottle tops, egg cartons, toilet rolls and anything else that Metalmiss could find.

'Don't miss this great experience!' Billy Bates was

yelling. 'Collage by robots. Potty collages by potty…'

'BILLY BATES!'

Billy jumped off the table as Mr Clegg strode into the room, followed by Professor Potter. 'Go to my room, boy. At once!'

Billy tried to look innocent. 'But why…?'

'You know why,' thundered Mr Clegg. 'This is a very serious matter. GO!'

Billy went.

Harry and Holly had never felt so pleased to see their grandpa. He walked over to Metalmiss, who was now slapping orange paint on to the egg boxes. He lifted a disc on her left shoulder and pressed something. She stood still.

Professor Potter smiled at the twins as he and Mr Clegg carried Metalmiss out of the room.

'Return to your own classroom, 3R,' said Mr Clegg. 'Miss Smith will take you for the rest of the day.'

When the children got home, Grandpa had already phoned.

'You were right, Harry,' said Mrs Potter. 'Billy Bates had interfered with the control box. You acted very sensibly. Grandpa was very proud of you.'

'Is Metalmiss badly damaged?' Harry asked anxiously.

'No,' said Mrs Potter. 'It will only take a day to repair her.'

'So she won't be there tomorrow.' Harry sounded disappointed.

'Why should you care?' Holly asked. 'I thought you didn't like Metalmiss.'

'So,' said Harry, 'I can change my mind, can't I?'

Chapter 9

3R were now so used to Metalmiss that even one day without her felt very strange. To his surprise, Harry found himself missing the sound of the robot's voice – the sound that he used to hate so much.

Billy Bates was not there but nobody missed him. He had been moved to another class and would not return to 3R. Harry felt pleased about that.

Next morning the twins bounced down to breakfast and gobbled up their cereal.

'Steady on,' said Mr Potter. 'What's got into you two?'

'Metalmiss is back,' they chorused.

'I thought Holly was the only Metalmiss fan in this house,' said Mr Potter. 'What happened to the boy who hated robots?'

Harry scowled. He did not want to be reminded about all that.

'He can change his mind if he wants to,' said Holly.

Harry looked at her gratefully. It wasn't often that Holly stood up for him like that.

The twins practically ran all the way to school and puffed into Room 6.

'Do not run,' said Metalmiss. 'Walk!'

There she was, at her desk, looking the same as ever. Harry sighed happily as she took the register, leaving out the name of Billy Bates.

'This afternoon,' announced Metalmiss, 'you will go to the hall to practise the play with Miss Bird.'

This year the school play was all about a beautiful princess who falls in love with a handsome woodcutter. The king and queen, naturally, do not want their daughter to marry a poor woodcutter. In the end, of course, he turns out to be a prince in disguise.

The fourth years had the main speaking parts and the best bits to play in the orchestra. As usual, to mop up the third years, there were masses of peasants, courtiers, musicians and ladies of the court.

Harry thought it was all very soppy but Holly loved it. She was a lady of the court and could wear a beautiful dress. Harry wasn't even a peasant. He and Rashid were part of the forest – a forest consisting of eight trees! To his disgust, he had to wear a pair of Holly's green tights and hold up a cardboard cut-out of a tree. At least no one could see his face!

The play was to be performed on the evening before the last day of term.

As the time approached, Miss Bird became more and more agitated. She was especially cross with 3R.

'How many times do I have to tell you that the peasants dance on from stage LEFT. Can't you tell left from right yet, third years? You are *not* supposed to crash into each other.'

One of the peasants dared to raise his hand.

'Yes?' said Miss Bird irritably.

'Wouldn't it be better, Miss, if the pheasants came on from...'

'PEASANTS!' screamed Miss Bird, 'not pheasants. And no. Whatever you were going to say, IT WOULD NOT BE BETTER. Go off stage, all of you, and come on again – properly.'

Now it was time for the forest scene, in which the handsome woodcutter appears.

The orchestra started to play...

'TREES!' yelled Miss Bird. 'Where are you, trees?'

The trees shuffled on.

'That was dreadful. Listen to the music. Try again.'

This time they came on properly, more or less.

'Is that Harry Potter's tree, bobbing about?'

Harry stuck his head round the side of his tree.

'Sorry, Miss Bird.'

'Miss Bird,' said Rashid helpfully, 'the trees could be swaying in the wind.'

Miss Bird gritted her teeth.

'There is no wind in this play, Rashid. And trees do not bob up and down, Harry. Keep your knees stiff.'

It was hard work holding a tree and *very* boring. Miss Bird should try it herself.

Holly's scene, of course, went perfectly.

'Well done, ladies of the court!' cried Miss Bird. 'Thank goodness someone is doing it properly.'

The ladies of the court tripped daintily off into the wings.

Harry was glad to get home. He threw down his schoolbag. 'I hate those stupid rehearsals. They're so boring.'

'I hear Miss Bird's feathers are getting ruffled,' said Mr Potter.

Harry did not laugh. 'It's horrible being a tree. My arms hurt from holding it up and Holly's tights are all scratchy.'

'I love being a lady of the court,' gushed Holly. 'Miss Bird said we were very good.'

'I thought you all looked very silly,' said Harry, 'in those stupid hats.'

'Not half as silly as your tree,' retorted Holly.

'Now, now,' said their mother soothingly. 'That's enough. I'm sure you'll both enjoy it on the night.'

'I won't,' said Harry gloomily. 'I'll hate it.'

On the evening of the performance the children had to return to school early for costumes and make-up. In the make-up room Lisa Jenkins, the beautiful princess, was protesting loudly.

'My mum says I'm allergic to stage make-up, Miss Bird. I'll come out in spots all over.'

But Miss Bird was firm. 'You're the beautiful princess, Lisa. You have to wear some make-up.'

'Ugh! I'm not kissing her if she's covered in spots,' said Andrew Marshall, who was the handsome woodcutter and prince.

'You're no oil painting yourself, Andrew Marshall,' said Lisa. 'So shut up.'

Miss Bird sighed. At least they were all here. That was something.

Harry didn't need any make-up. He put on his costume and went straight to Room 6. Metalmiss was sitting at her desk, looking at a copy of the play.

'I bet you know it all off by heart, Metalmiss.'

'Yes, Harry, I do know it. I am prompting.'

'Do you remember *everything* you read?'

'Yes, everything.'

'Wish I did,' said Harry enviously.

An excited bunch of peasants and courtiers crowded into the room. Before long they were all ready. It was time for the performance to begin. They could hear the opening music. The peasants were called.

Harry felt a tightening at the pit of his stomach. Even trees have feelings. His parents and grandparents were coming to see the play. They would not be looking at the handsome woodcutter.

90

They would be looking at his tree.

There was loud clapping. The peasants came back. They had been a success. Now it was a scene involving the king and queen and princess.

Mr Roberts put his head round the door. 'Trees,' he hissed. 'Backstage, please. You're next.'

They hurried down, collected their trees and tiptoed to the back of the stage. The woodcutter was there already.

The king and queen sang a duet. Everyone clapped. The princess stepped forward.

'You are cruel, father. You know that I love...aaah!'

Lisa screamed sharply as she tripped over her long skirt and pitched forward, hitting her head on the arm of the throne.

Miss Bird rushed on from the wings. Mr Clegg and Rashid's father, who was a doctor, climbed up the steps on to the stage. The curtains were quickly closed and the orchestra started to play.

Lisa needed a few stitches and Rashid's father offered to take her to casualty at once.

Backstage there was panic.

'What can we do?' moaned Miss Bird. 'We don't have an understudy. No one else knows the part.'

But there *was* someone who knew the part, who knew every part.

Harry rushed across the stage.

'Miss Bird,' he gabbled. 'Metalmiss. She knows the whole play by heart.'

'Oh, don't be silly,' said Miss Bird irritably. 'How could she ever look like a beautiful princess?'

'It might be worth trying,' said Mr Clegg.

'It's ruined anyway,' sighed Miss Bird. 'We've got nothing to lose, I suppose.'

Mr Clegg told the audience that Lisa would be all right and that a visiting actress would be taking her part.

'Metalmiss!' scowled Andrew Marshall. 'That's even worse than Lisa. I'm not kissing *her*. That's for sure.'

'Sssh!' whispered Harry. 'We're on now.'

As the trees trotted on, Harry felt quite pleased with himself. He stood stiff and straight, knowing that he was being watched. For some reason the handsome woodcutter was not on top form. He forgot his lines – twice.

The audience gasped as Metalmiss stepped on to the stage. She did not look like Lisa Jenkins but she did look strangely beautiful. On her cap and on her tunic every disc was glowing. She shone with a mysterious blue-green light. Even the metallic voice seemed softer, though it carried clearly to the back of the hall.

'My father wants me to marry Prince Albert, woodcutter. What shall I do?'

As Andrew stared at Metalmiss, he forgot about the audience. He stood up straight. He spoke out. He was every inch a prince.

Miss Bird had often complained about the stage lighting. She did not need to now. Whenever Metalmiss stepped from the wings, the whole stage lit up.

In the bleak mid-winter scene the peasants shivered in a cold, ice blue light. In the garden scene the princess's tunic and cap glowed with a rich, golden yellow. Even the paper flowers and shrubs looked real and beautiful.

The audience watched, entranced.

'Magic,' one man was heard to murmur. 'Pure magic.'

The children felt happy and confident. They enjoyed every minute. They had never acted so well.

'Amazing,' Miss Bird kept saying over and over. 'Simply amazing.'

The wedding scene was the climax of the play. Every disc on the bride's tunic and cap gleamed like the purest silver and all the children were bathed in a strange, silvery light. Metalmiss *did* look like a princess – an alien princess, from another world.

Then it was all over. They were taking their bow.

The audience stood and cheered and clapped as if they would never stop.

Mr Clegg stepped forward. He thanked everyone

for their hard work.

'Finally,' he said, 'I would like to congratuate our beautiful princess on a performançe that one can only call – dazzling.'

'Metalmiss,' chanted the audience. 'Metalmiss.'

They cheered wildly as the curtains opened and Metalmiss stepped forward and bowed once more.

'Bet you felt proud of Metalmiss, Grandpa,' said Holly as they drove home.

'Yes, of course,' said Grandpa. 'But I did notice a very beautiful lady of the court and a very fine tree in the forest.'

Chapter 10

The play was over. It was the last day of term. School would break up at lunch time and then the long summer holiday would stretch ahead – weeks and weeks of it.

The twins tried to think of all that as they dragged along the street to school. But their hearts and their legs felt heavy. They could only think of one thing, something they had almost forgotten in the excitement of the play. Today they would have to say goodbye to Metalmiss.

As they filed into the hall, Harry remembered that other assembly, at the beginning of term. It seemed a long time ago. As they looked at the grey, metallic figure on the platform, he wondered how he could ever have hated her so much.

'And now,' Mr Clegg was saying, 'it only remains for me to bid farewell to Metalmiss. I think we would all agree that her stay with us has been most successful. I cannot thank you enough, Metalmiss, for all that you have done for the school, and for 3R.'

Metalmiss stepped forward.

'Thank you, Headmaster. I too am pleased that our experiment has been a success. But there is no need for thanks. It is what I am programmed to do.'

As she said the familiar words, Harry looked

round at Holly. This time they did not laugh. Harry could see that Holly's eyes were filling up with tears. Quickly, he looked away.

Then Mr Jones led three cheers for Metalmiss and the children trooped out of the hall.

Back in Room 6 Metalmiss took the register as usual.

'Now,' she announced. 'I have brought some games for you to play on the screen. There is a small control box for each of you.'

Each little box, about the size of a matchbox, had a number on it and four buttons. Harry's was number 10.

'The first game is called "Magic Maze" . On the screen you can see a maze. There is a small ring with your number. Use the buttons to guide your ring out of the maze.'

Because it was such a big screen they could all play at once. Rashid was the first to get his ring out of the maze.

There were lots of games. They were all good fun. The children were so busy that the morning was over before they had time to think.

'It is now 12.30,' announced Metalmiss. 'Time to go home.'

The children looked at each other. They all felt the same.

'Can't you stay at this school, Metalmiss?' Sally

blurted, on the verge of tears. 'We don't want you to go.'

'Do you *have* to leave?' asked Rashid. 'You have been my most interesting teacher.'

Metalmiss stood up.

'Yes,' she said firmly. 'The experiment is over. I have to go.'

'She doesn't understand how we feel,' Sally whispered to Holly.

'No,' said Holly. 'Sometimes I wish she could turn into a real person.'

As Metalmiss gazed at 3R, her blue eyes slowly changed to that soft, glowing yellow. The children no longer felt sad. They felt happy and calm. They began to dream of sunny beaches, of the long summer holiday.

'It is time to go home now, 3R. You have worked hard this term. Goodbye and enjoy your holiday.'

'Goodbye, Metalmiss,' they chanted. 'Goodbye.'

Holly and Harry were almost home when Harry remembered.

'My school report. I've left it on the desk. I'd better go back for it.'

'Not again!' groaned Holly. 'You'd forget your head if it wasn't screwed on.'

Outside Room 6, Harry hesitated. The door was closed. Metalmiss was sitting at her desk.

As Harry opened the door she slowly turned

her head.

'I've forgotten my report, Metalmiss.'

'Yes, Harry. It is on your desk.'

The classroom clock ticked loudly. Harry had never heard it before.

'It's very quiet,' he said as he collected his report, 'without 3R.'

'Yes,' said Metalmiss. 'Very quiet. I am waiting for Professor Potter.'

'Goodbye, Metalmiss,' said Harry.

As he left the room he added, almost under his breath, 'I'll miss you.'

'Goodbye, Harry.'

As he closed the door, Harry took one last look at Metalmiss. She was sitting absolutely still, staring straight ahead.

Harry blinked and looked again. He could have sworn that a tear rolled gently down one metallic cheek and plopped on to the desk.

He walked slowly down the corridor, thinking. Of course, that was impossible.

It must have been his imagination.

A trick of the light?

A drop of oil?

One of those things. For no robot, not even Metalmiss, has ever felt happy or ever felt sad.

Other great reads ✦ *from* **Red Fox**

Further Red Fox titles that you might enjoy reading are listed on the following pages. They are available in bookshops or they can be ordered directly from us.

If you would like to order books, please send this form and the money due to:

ARROW BOOKS, BOOKSERVICE BY POST, PO BOX 29, DOUGLAS, ISLE OF MAN, BRITISH ISLES. Please enclose a cheque or postal order made out to Arrow Books Ltd for the amount due, plus 75p per book for postage and packing to a maximum of £7.50, both for orders within the UK. For customers outside the UK, please allow £1.00 per book.

NAME_____

ADDRESS_____

_____

Please print clearly.

Whilst every effort is made to keep prices low, it is sometimes necessary to increase cover prices at short notice. If you are ordering books by post, to save delay it is advisable to phone to confirm the correct price. The number to ring is THE SALES DEPARTMENT 071 (if outside London) 973 9700.

Other great reads ⬿ *from* **Red Fox**

Discover the great animal stories of Colin Dann

JUST NUFFIN

The Summer holidays loomed ahead with nothing to look forward to except one dreary week in a caravan with only Mum and Dad for company. Roger was sure he'd be bored.

But then Dad finds Nuffin: an abandoned puppy who's more a bundle of skin and bones than a dog. Roger's holiday is transformed and he and Nuffin are inseparable. But Dad is adamant that Nuffin must find a new home. Is there *any* way Roger can persuade him to change his mind?

ISBN 0 09 966900 5   £2.99

KING OF THE VAGABONDS

'You're very young,' Sammy's mother said, 'so heed my advice. Don't go into Quartermile Field.'

His mother and sister are happily domesticated but Sammy, the tabby cat, feels different. They are content with their lot, never wondering what lies beyond their immediate surroundings. But Sammy is burningly curious and his life seems full of mysteries. Who is his father? Where has he gone? And what is the mystery of Quartermile Field?

ISBN 0 09 957190 0   £2.99

OTHER TITLES YOU MAY ENJOY FROM RED FOX

☐ The Seven Treasure Hunts	Betsy Byars	£2.50
☐ Flossie Teacake's Fur Coat	Hunter Davies	£2.99
☐ The House that Sailed Away	Pat Hutchins	£2.99
☐ Rats!	Pat Hutchins	£2.99
☐ Burping Bertha	Michael Rosen	£2.50
☐ Who's Afraid of the Evil Eye?	Hazel Townson	£2.50
☐ Lenny and Jake Adventures	Hazel Townson	£2.99

PRICES AND OTHER DETAILS ARE LIABLE TO CHANGE

ARROW BOOKS, BOOKSERVICE BY POST, PO BOX 29, DOUGLAS, ISLE OF MAN, BRITISH ISLES

NAME...

ADDRESS ....

....

....

Please enclose a cheque or postal order made out to B.S.B.P. Ltd. for the amount due and allow the following for postage and packing:

U.K. CUSTOMERS: Please allow 75p per book to a maximum of £7.50

B.F.P.O. & EIRE: Please allow 75p per book to a maximum of £7.50

OVERSEAS CUSTOMERS: Please allow £1.00 per book.

While every effort is made to keep prices low it is sometimes necessary to increase cover prices at short notice. Arrow Books reserve the right to show new retail prices on covers which may differ from those previously advertised in the text or elsewhere.

Have a chuckle with Red Fox Fiction!

FLOSSIE TEACAKE'S FUR COAT   Hunter Davies

Flossie just wants to be grown-up, like her big sister Bella – and when she tries on the mysterious fur coat she finds in Bella's bedroom, her wildest dreams come true . . .
ISBN 0 09 996710 3   £2.99

SNOTTY BUMSTEAD   Hunter Davies

Snotty's mum has gone away leaving him with lots of cash and the house to himself! Burgers for breakfast, football in the front room – and no homework! But can he keep the nosey grown-ups away?
ISBN 0 09 997710 9   £2.99

HENRY HOLLINS AND THE DINOSAUR
Willis Hall

Little did Henry think, when he found the fossilized egg at the seaside, that it was actually a fossilized DINOSAUR egg! He had even less idea that it would be no time at all before he would be travelling up the moorway on a dinosaur's back!
ISBN 0 09 911611 1   £2.99

THE LAST VAMPIRE   Willis Hall

The Hollins family are on holiday in Europe, and all goes well until they stay the night in a spooky castle, miles from nowhere. Even worse, they discover that they are in the castle belonging to Count Alucard.
ISBN 0 09 911541 7   £2.99

TRIV IN PURSUIT   Michael Coleman

One by one, the teachers at St Ethelred's School are vanishing, leaving cryptic notes behind. "Triv" Trevellyan smells something fishy going on and is determined to find out just what is happening!
ISBN 0 09 991660 6   £2.99

Other great reads ← *from* **Red Fox**

Action-Packed Drama with Red Fox Fiction!

SIMPLE SIMON   Yvonne Coppard

Simon isn't stupid – he's just not very good at practical things. So when Mum collapses, it's Cara, his younger sister who calls the ambulance and keeps a cool head. Simon plans to show what he can do too, in a crisis, but his plan goes frighteningly wrong . . .
ISBN 0 09 910531 4   £2.99

LOW TIDE   William Mayne
Winner of the Guardian Children's Fiction Award.

The low tide at Jade Bay leaves fish on dry land and a wreck high on a rock. Is this the treasure ship the divers have been looking for? Three friends vow to find out – and find themselves swept away into adventure.
ISBN 0 09 918311 0   £3.50

THE INTRUDER   John Rowe Townsend

It isn't often that you meet someone who claims to be you. But that's what happens to Arnold Haithwaite. The real Arnold has to confront the menacing intruder before he takes over his life completely.
ISBN 0 09 999260 4   £3.50

GUILTY   Ruth Thomas

Everyone in Kate's class says that the local burglaries have been done by Desmond Locke's dad, because he's just come out of prison. Kate and Desmond think otherwise and set out to prove who really is *guilty*.
ISBN 0 09 918591 1   £2.99

Other great reads from **Red Fox**

School stories from Enid Blyton

THE NAUGHTIEST GIRL IN THE SCHOOL

Elizabeth knows that she's going to hate boarding school and decides that the only way to get out of it is to be so naughty that she's sent straight home again. So she sets out to do just that – stirring up all sorts of trouble and getting herself the name of the bold bad schoolgirl. She's sure all she wants is to go home again, until she realises, to her surprise, that there are some things she hadn't reckoned with. Like making friends . . .

ISBN 0 09 945500 5   £2.99

THE NAUGHTIEST GIRL AGAIN

Elizabeth Allen is back at school for her second term and this time she's *not* going to be the naughtiest girl in the school any more . . . or so she thinks. It isn't as easy as all that though, and it seems that even when she's trying to be good, things still keep going wrong. So who is Elizabeth's secret enemy who wants her to get in trouble?

ISBN 0 09 915911 2   £2.99

THE NAUGHTIEST GIRL IS A MONITOR

Third term at Whyteleafe and to her surprise, Elizabeth is chosen to be a monitor. She tries her very best to set a good example to the other children but somehow things go wrong for her and soon she is in just as much trouble as she was in her first term, when she was the naughtiest girl in the school!

ISBN 0 09 945490 4   £2.99

Other great reads ✧ *from* **Red Fox**

Enter the magical world of Dr Dolittle

Dr Dolittle is one of the great book characters – everyone knows the kindly doctor who can talk to the animals. With his household of animals – Too-Too the owl, Dab-Dab the duck, Gub-gub the pig and Jip the dog – and Tommy Stubbins, his assistant, he finds himself in and out of trouble, of money and of England in a series of adventures. These editions have been sensitively edited with the approval of Christopher Lofting, the author's son.

THE STORY OF DOCTOR DOLITTLE
ISBN 0 09 985470 8   £3.99

THE VOYAGES OF DOCTOR DOLITTLE
ISBN 0 09 985470 8   £4.99

DR DOLITTLE'S POST OFFICE
ISBN 0 09 988040 7   £4.99

DR DOLITTLE'S CIRCUS
ISBN 0 09 985440 6   £4.99

DR DOLITTLE'S ZOO
ISBN 0 09 988030 X   £4.99

DR DOLITTLE'S GARDEN
ISBN 0 09 988050 4   £4.99

DR DOLITTLE IN THE MOON
ISBN 0 09 988060 1   £4.99

DR DOLITTLE'S CARAVAN
ISBN 0 09 985450 3   £4.99

DR DOLITTLE AND THE GREEN CANARY
ISBN 0 09 988090 3   £4.99

Other great reads ✎ *from* **Red Fox**

Discover the hilarious world of Red Fox younger fiction!

ALIENS FOR BREAKFAST   Jonathan Etra and Stephanie Spinner

Richard's new cereal is *really* exciting – it contains Aric who has been beamed down from another planet to save the Earth from alien invasion.

ISBN 0 09 981550 8   £2.25

BILLY AND THE GHASTLY GHOST   Mick Gowar

Billy is convinced he has seen a ghost in the graveyard – but proving it to the rest of his class is difficult.

ISBN 0 09 981490 0   £2.99

BILLY AND THE MAN-EATING PLANT
Mick Gower

Billy has to come up with a prizewinning project for the class prize – but he never seems to have the time.

ISBN 0 09 981500 1   £2.50

THANKS FOR THE SARDINE   Laura Beaumont

Aggie decides that her boring Aunts need reforming so she arranges for them to have some training.

ISBN 0 09 997900 4   £2.99

MERVYN'S REVENGE   Leone Peguero

Mervyn the cat is outraged when his family go away without him, and he plots revenge with feline cunning.

ISBN 0 09 997520 3   £2.50

Other great reads *from* **Red Fox**

Have some supernatural fun with Jonathan's ghost

Dave is just an ordinary schoolboy – except he happens to be a ghost, and only his friend, Jonathan, can see him. With his love of mischief, Dave creates quite a bit of trouble for Jonathan to explain away – but he can also be an extremely useful friend to have when Jonathan's in a fix.

JONATHAN'S GHOST

Jonathan's starting at a new school – but who needs humans when you've got a ghost for a friend?

ISBN 0 09 968850 6   £2.50

SPITFIRE SUMMER

An old wartime ghost seems to be haunting Jonathan – and only Dave can help him.

ISBN 0 09 968850 6   £2.50

THE SCHOOL SPIRIT

A trip to an old mansion brings Jonathan into contact with a triangle of evil determined to find a new victim.

ISBN 0 09 974620 4   £2.50

JONATHAN AND THE SUPERSTAR

Everyone at Jonathan's school thinks Jason Smythe is wonderful – except Dave. Dave senses trouble afoot . . .

ISBN 0 09 995120 7   £2.50

Other great reads from **Red Fox**

Discover the wacky world of Spacedog and Roy by Natalie Standiford

Spacedog isn't really a dog at all – he's an alien lifeform from the planet Queekrg, who just happens to *look* like a dog. It's a handy form of disguise – but he's not sure he'll *ever* get used to the food!

SPACEDOG AND ROY

Roy is quite surprised to find an alien spacecraft in his garden – but that's nothing to the surprise he gets when Spacedog climbs out.

ISBN 0 09 983650 5   £2.99

SPACEDOG AND THE PET SHOW

Life becomes unbearable for Spacedog when he's entered for the local pet show and a French poodle falls in love with him.

ISBN 0 09 983660 2   £2.99

SPACEDOG IN TROUBLE

When Spacedog is mistaken for a stray and locked up in the animal santuary, he knows he's in big trouble.

ISBN 0 09 983670 X   £2.99

SPACEDOG THE HERO

When Roy's father goes away he makes Spacedog the family watchdog – but Spacedog is scared of the dark. What can he do?

ISBN 0 09 983680 7   £2.99

Other great reads ✦ *from* **Red Fox**

Have a bundle of fun with the wonderful Pat Hutchins

Pat Hutchins' stories are full of wild adventure and packed with outrageous humour for younger readers to enjoy.

FOLLOW THAT BUS

A school party visit to a farm ends in chaotic comedy when two robbers steal the school bus.

ISBN 0 09 993220 2   £2.99

THE HOUSE THAT SAILED AWAY

An hilarious story of a family afloat, in their house, in the Pacific Ocean. No matter what adventures arrive, Gran always has a way to deal with them.

ISBN 0 09 993200 8   £2.99

RATS!

Sam's ploys to persuade his parents to let him have a pet rat eventually meet with success, and with Nibbles in the house, life is never the same again.

ISBN 0 09 993190 7   £2.50

Join the RED FOX Reader's Club

The Red Fox Reader's Club is for readers of all ages. All you have to do is ask your local bookseller or librarian for a Red Fox Reader's Club card. As an official Red Fox Reader you only have to borrow or buy eight Red Fox books in order to qualify for your own Red Fox Reader's Clubpack – full of exciting surprises! If you have any difficulty obtaining a Red Fox Reader's Club card please write to: Random House Children's Books Marketing Department, 20 Vauxhall Bridge Road, London SW1V 2SA.